Piccolo Adventure Library
King Solomon's Mines

Piccolo Adventure Library

King Solomon's Mines

retold by Alan Robertshaw from the original by Rider Haggard
text and cover illustrations by Tom Barling
Piccolo Original Pan Books

First published 1977 by Pan Books Ltd,
Cavaye Place, London SW10 9PG
2nd printing 1978
Text © Pan Books Ltd 1977
Illustrations © Tom Barling 1977
ISBN 0 330 25133 3
Printed and bound in Great Britain by
Richard Clay (The Chaucer Press) Ltd, Bungay, Suffolk

Contents

1 A legend unfolds   7
2 The journey begins   18
3 Thirst and hunger   31
4 Taken by surprise   40
5 The king   48
6 Death dance   55
7 Hill battle   66
8 The mines at last   83
9 Back from the dead   96

1 A legend unfolds

I suppose it must always be difficult to know how to begin
a story, and for an old elephant hunter like me it is
especially hard. I am more used to handling a rifle than a
pen. Still, I have told Sir Henry Curtis and Captain Good
that I will try to write down our extraordinary adventures
in a good, plain way. So I had better make a start.

Strange that our adventures, which were in deserts,
across mountains, and in the depths of the earth, should
have begun at sea. I – my name is Allan Quatermain, by
the way – was taking ship from Durban to Natal. I had
been ill with a fever which I had caught on my last hunting
expedition, and was eager to get back to the great plains
of Southern Africa. The ship was the *S.S. Dunkeld*, and
I remember there were only a few passengers. But however
many there had been, I should have noticed Sir Henry
Curtis. He was a big man – not just tall, but big in every
way. Powerful arms, fine broad shoulders, and a head
like a lion's – yellow hair, yellow beard and deep grey eyes.

He was talking earnestly and quietly at the dinner table
one night with his companion, Captain Good. The
Captain was a merry little man with a monocle – and, as I
was to find out, false teeth. But that all belongs to a later
part of the story. He and Sir Henry were asking many
questions about Africa, and at last their conversation

turned to elephants. 'Ah,' said someone further down the table. 'You want to ask Hunter Quatermain about elephants. He knows more about them than any man.'

Sir Henry seemed to start at the mention of my name, but he said no more until after dinner. Then, as I was leaving the dining saloon, his deep voice stopped me. 'Excuse me, but is your name Allan Quatermain?' I nodded, and to my surprise found myself invited down to the big man's cabin. A bottle of whisky was brought out and poured. Then we spent several minutes lighting our pipes. And all the time my curiosity was growing.

At last Sir Henry leaned forward and asked me whether I had been at a place called Bamangwatto about two years ago, and whether I had met there a young Englishman called Neville.

'Why, yes,' I said. I was surprised that he should know so much about my movements. 'The young man was equipping himself for an expedition to the North. He meant to take a wagon to the edge of the Matabele country, then to sell it and go on foot. And I believe he did so,' I went on, remembering more of the young man. 'I saw his wagon later with a trader who said he had bought it from him.'

'Mr. Quatermain,' said Sir Henry, 'I must ask whether

you knew the purpose of Mr. Neville's journey.'

I paused. I did indeed know, but it was not a subject I cared to discuss. 'Perhaps I heard something,' I answered vaguely.

Sir Henry's grey eyes looked at me keenly for a moment. Then he sighed and those eyes seemed to cloud over with some painful memory. 'I see I must trust you with more of my story, before I can ask you to trust me with yours,' he said at last. 'Mr. Neville, you see, is my brother.'

Then he told me the story of perhaps the only mean act of his life. It seemed that when his father died, Sir Henry inherited the family fortune, as well as his title. Unfortunately he and his brother, who had always been the best of friends, had quarrelled. I think it was over a woman, but that hardly matters. His brother, George, had taken it that this quarrel would leave him penniless; and Sir Henry had left it too late to tell him this was not so. For George, taking the name of Neville, had left for Africa to make his fortune.

All that was two years ago; and George Curtis, alias Neville, had not been heard of since. 'In fact,' went on Sir Henry, 'you, Mr. Quatermain, were the last white man to see my brother. Perhaps you can understand now why I must find out all I can about his plans. If he is still alive I, and the Captain here, who has offered his help, must find him.'

'Yes,' agreed Captain Good, who had watched his friend anxiously. 'So if you have any idea where George Curtis was going, please tell us.'

'I believe,' I said, 'though I have never mentioned it to a soul until this day, that your brother was looking for King Solomon's Mines.'

'King Solomon's Mines!' they both exclaimed. 'And where in the world are they?'

'I don't know,' I had to tell them, honestly. 'But I may have a better idea of where they are than anyone else. Listen. I will tell you all I know about them, but you must both promise to keep secret what I say.'

They agreed, and I then told them a story I had never told anyone since it happened, more than fifteen years ago.

About that time I had been hunting way up north of the Matabele country. It had been a bad hunt, and I ended by catching a bad fever. For two or three months I was laid up in an African village called Sitanda's Kraal, and while I was there a strange little man passed through the Kraal.

He was a Portuguese called José Silvestre, a tall, dark man with moustachios. I was still very ill when he came to the place for the first time, but he looked in on me when he heard there was a sick white man in the Kraal.

When he left he said, 'Goodbye, senor. If ever we meet again I shall be the richest man in the world.' Then he just walked off into the great desert that lay to the West. I remember watching him walk away as the sun set behind the tips of the mountains that lay many miles distant on the furthest edge of the desert – they call them the Suliman mountains. I thought he must have been mad.

I never expected to see him again, but one day a week or so later, when I was well enough to walk about a bit, I saw something moving out on the edge of the desert. I watched for a while as it moved and stopped, moved and stopped. Then I realised it was a man crawling along.

I sent one of my hunters out at once to help the poor creature, and who should he bring back but José Silvestre. Or what was left of him. The man was little more than a skeleton. His face was yellow with fever, his eyes had sunk deep into their sockets. Through cracked lips he feebly whispered, 'Water! Water!'

We took him back to the Kraal and did what we could for him, but it was hopeless. He raved half the night. I sat up with him and fed him a little milk when I could.

But at dawn a strange thing happened. As the first light of the sun struck across the desert and lit the peak of the mountains beyond, he sat up and pointed a wavering finger. 'There it is!' he cried weakly. 'But I shall never reach it! No-one will ever reach it!' Then he turned towards me. 'Friend,' he said. 'Are you there? My eyes grow dark.'

I took his hand. 'I am here,' I said. 'But lie back and rest.'

'There will be time enough to rest soon,' he answered. 'I am dying. But you have been good to me. I will give you the paper. Perhaps you can cross the desert that has killed me.' He reached inside his shirt and passed me a little leather wallet. His fingers were too feeble to open it. 'Look inside,' he went on. His voice was growing weak. 'It was written three hundred years ago by an ancestor of mine. He was José Silvestre, too. And he died, as I will, seeking King Solomon's treasure.' He paused and the flicker of a grim smile moved his face. Then he grew urgent, gripping my arm. 'Take the paper. Take the map. Go yourself, friend. Perhaps you will be the richest man in the world.'

After that he said nothing, and before the sun was fully risen, he died.

Sir Henry, when he had heard my story, was very excited. 'But what about the paper, man?' he asked impatiently. 'What was in it?'

'The original was written in the dying man's blood on a torn scrap of his own clothing,' I said. 'I keep it at home. But I have an English translation of it, and a copy of the map that was with it, here in my wallet.' I took it out and Sir Henry and Captain Good crowded round me to read it. This is what it said:

'I, José da Silvestra, write this. I am dying of hunger in a cave near the peak of the southernmost of the two mountains I have named Sheba's Breasts. If my servant comes for me he will find this. Then, if any man comes after me, let him climb the left Breast of Sheba. Let him follow King Solomon's road which runs from the north side of that mountain, and let him find the Treasure House of King Solomon's Mines, which I have seen with mine own eyes. But let him beware of the savage customs of the Kukuana people, and most let him beware of Gagool.'

The letter was signed, and with it was a map.

When they had read the letter and studied the map, both Sir Henry and Captain Good sat back and looked at me. 'Well,' said the Captain at last, 'I've travelled further and seen more things than most men – but I've never heard anything like this.'

'Nor have I,' said Sir Henry. 'You're quite sure of all this, Mr. Quatermain?'

I am not used to men doubting my word, and I said so.

'But how does this affect my brother?' asked Sir Henry.

I went on with my story. 'On the night before Mr. Neville – as I knew him – set out, I saw the native hunter he had hired to go with him. He was an old African called Jim. I knew him well. "Jim," I asked him, "where are you and the Englishman going?"

'"Ah, we're off to the Suliman Mountains to seek our fortune," he answered. "Mr. Neville reckons that is

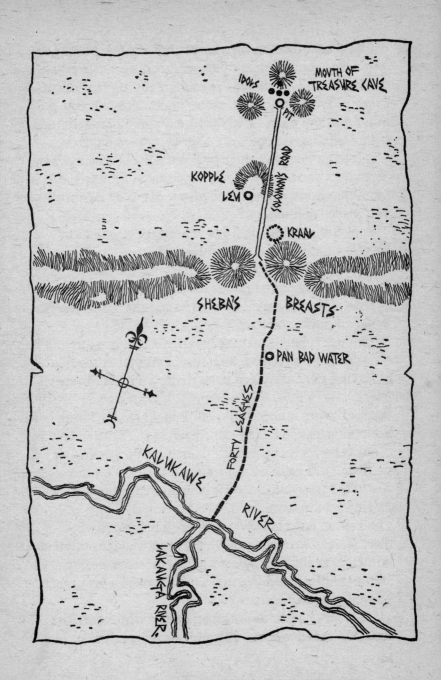

where King Solomon kept his diamond mines."

' "Then you are mad to go with him, Jim," I told him.
"You'll both be food for vultures if you try to cross that
desert." But I could see that he was as determined to go
as his master. Then I had the idea that it might help them
if I jotted down some of the directions from old Don
José's letter and gave them to Jim. "Mind," I said, when
I gave him the paper, "I don't want to be pestered with a
lot of questions, so don't you give it Mr. Neville until
you're well on the way."

'So you see, gentlemen, I have a pretty clear idea of
exactly where George Curtis was going.'

'Mr. Quatermain,' said Sir Henry, when I had
finished, 'I intend to find my brother, wherever he is.
I see that you are a man that our expedition badly needs.
Will you come with me?'

I smiled. 'Thank you very much, Sir Henry – but that is
an invitation I shall have to refuse. I am rather too fond
of staying alive to try and cross to the Suliman Mountains.'

I tried to put it cheerfully, but I could see they were both
disappointed. Sir Henry leaned across the little cabin table
towards me, and tried again. 'I am not a poor man,' he
said, 'and this expedition means a lot to me. Within reason
you may name your price for being our guide – and I will
pay the sum in advance.'

Now I am not a greedy man – nor a brave one – but
these were generous terms Sir Henry was offering. I had
hunted elephants all my life without growing wealthy
on the profits. And I had a son at home who I very much
wanted to provide for.

'Sir Henry,' I said at last, 'I still think whoever tries to
reach the mines will die. But your offer is tempting. Let

me think about it for a day or two.'

And, of course, when he came up to me as the 'Dunkeld' was docking in Natal, and asked for my decision, I said I would go.

2 The journey begins

Once I had decided to go with them, I set about preparing for the expedition with a will. It was not that I had changed my mind. I still thought none of us could ever survive the journey. But since I was to risk my life, I decided to have every advantage money could buy. I picked out the best covered wagon in Natal, with a team of fine Zulu oxen to pull it. As well as revolvers and hunting guns – the usual things for an elephant shoot – I bought three fine rifles and enough ammunition for an army. We also had medicines, supplies of food, blankets – in fact it was the best-equipped expedition that ever left Natal.

We had fine native servants with us, too. One was a wiry little Hottentot, a man called Ventvögel. I had hunted with him before, and I knew no finer tracker. The other – well, the other was Umbopa. He was no Hottentot, nor had I ever seen him before he appeared silently before me one day, bowed, and said, 'Macumazahn, I hear you go on a long trek beyond the Suliman Mountains.'

I looked up at him – for he was a huge man, taller than a Zulu, with a glossy, black skin. 'What is it to you where I go?' I asked him. I was suspicious of a stranger who seemed to know so much about me. He even knew the name my own hunters called me – Macumazahn. It meant

'Man who does not sleep', or 'The watchful one'.

Umbopa did not seem at all put out, but bowed
politely. 'It has this to do with me, Macumazahn. If you
go that way, I would come with you.'

Now I am used to hiring my own servants, not having
them hire me! I was just about to send the man away,
when Sir Henry spoke. 'What does the man want?' I
translated Umbopa's words, and Sir Henry said, 'Ask
him why he wants to come with us.'

I put the question, and Umbopa answered calmly,
'I come from the North and now I am tired of this country.
I would go back. I am a strong man and a good hunter.

I will earn my keep.' He said this with a simple dignity, then he stood up. 'That is all. Umbopa has spoken.'

Sir Henry did not wait for me to translate the answer. 'Let him come with us,' he said, and stood facing him.

It struck me at once how well matched they were in build. Both stood over six feet. Both were powerful men.

It seemed to strike Umbopa, too, for he looked straight at Sir Henry and said, 'It is well. We are men, you and I.'

I had never met an African servant like him before, and I can't say I really trusted him even then. But Sir Henry had spoken, and that was Sir Henry's business.

My business was to complete our preparations, and in less than a week we were ready to depart. And I must admit that, despite my certainty that we were on a fool's errand, it was a fine expedition that left Natal for the North.

We went up country like any other hunting party. No-one would have guessed the real purpose of the trip. Indeed I remember Captain Good – who, to be honest, was not very good with a gun – banging away at any game we met. He once, by some extraordinary chance, actually managed to hit a giraffe – and always afterwards seemed to think himself a great marksman!

It was a pleasant trip, and I had almost forgotten the grim adventure waiting for us at the end of it when we arrived at last at Sitanda's Kraal. The little village was the last before the great, sandy desert that divided us from the Suliman Mountains and what lay beyond. The three of us – Sir Henry, Good and myself – stood at the edge of the Kraal and gazed out over the shimmering heat. It was evening, I remember, and the sun seemed to be settling over the jagged, distant peaks. It was very beautiful.

'We are men, you and I'

We watched for a while in silence. Then Sir Henry spoke.

'So that is where my brother is. Well, there is no help for it. That is where we must look for him.'

'It is a far journey, white men,' said a voice behind us. I turned round and there was Umbopa, staring, like us, out across the desert. 'The desert is harsh and there is but little water. I ask myself why the Incubu wishes to go there.'

Incubu was the name the Africans had begun to give Sir Henry. It meant, I believe, 'The Elephant'. Personally, I did not like the big Zulu's tone of voice – but again Sir Henry answered him.

'Yes, it is far,' he said, 'but no journey is too far for a man looking for his brother.'

Umbopa's face took on a distant look. 'Perhaps I also seek a brother over the mountains,' he said, strangely.

Now my suspicions were even greater. 'What do you know about the land over the mountains?' I asked him, shortly.

He looked at me, and answered calmly, 'A little. And what I do know I will tell if we ever get there. But it is a land of danger, white men – danger and strange customs. Take my warning and do not go. I have spoken.'

With these strange words he saluted with his spear, turned on his heel, and was gone. And when I next saw him he was sitting cleaning a rifle like any other African servant.

Still, I had little enough time to worry about Umbopa's strange words, for there was now much to be done. All our gear had to be left behind and looked after, except what we could carry on our backs – and I was afraid it might be tampered with. I found an old African who agreed to take care of the stuff; then I loaded all the guns we were not taking with us and laid them out on the sand.

'These,' I said to the old fellow, 'are live Devils, and you must not touch them.' Then I stood back and waited.

Sure enough, the old fellow could not resist the temptation. He picked up an elephant gun – and blew a hole clean through one of his own oxen!

After that I felt sure our belongings would be safe.

The last problem was to decide what we would – or rather what we could – take with us. We were crossing a vast and waterless desert, and passing on into unknown country. We would need both food and water as well as blankets and guns. Yet if we tried to carry too much, we knew we would never even cross the desert.

At last we fixed on four pints of water each, and five pounds of biltong – the dried meat that hunters carry. It was not much; but as we all shouldered our packs, they felt heavy enough to carry across the terrible country in front of us.

It was moonrise when we set off – for we hoped to be able to cover many miles before the heat of the sun was on us. Umbopa stood a little way ahead of us, staring into the dark of the desert, while Sir Henry turned to Good and myself. 'Gentlemen,' he said, 'it is a strange journey we are going on, and none of us knows if we will ever come back. But a man could not wish for two truer friends to be with him.'

And with that we moved off into the desert.

We had nothing to see by but the dim moon – nothing to guide us but the rough map of a dying man. It seemed a madman's journey. And the desert was determined that not one step of it should be easy. The thorny bushes that

clung to the barren earth caught at our ankles. Sand got
into our veldschoon – the soft hunting shoes we had
chosen to walk in. Even Captain Good, who always liked
to look smart, found the grit in his shiny leather boots.

And the desert seemed filled with a great, lonely
silence. It wrapped itself round our heads as we walked,
muffling even the tread of our feet. Once someone ahead
of me began to whistle, but after a few bars the tune
faded away. It only made the silence seem deeper.

Then, just when it seemed that nothing could disturb
the quiet of the desert, the most extraordinary thing
happened. Good had been leading with the compass –

26

which he as a sailor understood – and the rest of us were walking behind in single file. Then suddenly there was a cry and Good vanished. The next second, the night was full of snorts, bellows and thundering hooves. Great shapes blundered by us in the night. Imagine our surprise when we suddenly saw Good on the back of one of them, being carried off towards the mountains!

Luckily before he had gone far he tumbled to the earth with a thump. We rushed to him and found him winded but unhurt. Apparently he had walked right into a herd of sleeping quagga – creatures something like a zebra – and before he could do anything to save himself, he had fallen onto one of their backs!

The rest of the night passed without incident and we were able to walk on into the morning, until the heat of the sun forced us to shelter under a large rock. There we slept, and the next night we walked again. I think we should have crossed the desert quite easily if we had been able to go on like this. But the morning after that, the sun came up to show a bare and barren scene. There was neither tree nor rock to shelter us. No-one who has never spent a day in such heat can imagine what it is like. At first we lay flat, and drank a little. Then we sat, and drank a little. Still too hot, we scraped out little hollows and baked in them for a while. And we drank a little. At last we gave up any thought of rest and staggered on into the blinding afternoon sun.

Towards evening, exhausted and tortured by heat and thirst, we came to a low hill. On its slopes we lay down, sucked the last drops of our precious water from the bottles, and slept. As I shut my eyes I heard Umbopa say, 'If we cannot find water tomorrow, we will die.'

Old Don José's map had marked a water hole out in the

desert, and by our reckoning we should have been close to it. But neither at night when we lay down, nor in the morning when we rose, could we see any sign of the valley or the trees that would show it to us.

For a moment at sunrise, though, we saw a sight that took our minds off even the thought of water. There, in the pink light of dawn, two beautiful rounded mountains towered up from the solid wall of the Suliman Mountains. The snow gleamed for a while on the peaks Don José had called Sheba's Breasts – then, like a veil, the cloud came down over them.

We had seen our goal. But without water we would never reach it.

Our lips cracked and peeled. The sun beat at us. The little hill gave no shade, and our eyes smarted as we strained them for any sign of water. I think we would have given up hope if Ventvögel had not found the tracks of a herd of springbok. We knew that where there were springbok there had to be water.

All the same, we walked round and round that hill, and all the horizon would show us was sand.

'But I smell water,' Ventvögel insisted.

'Perhaps it is on top of the hill,' suggested Sir Henry.

'Rot,' I answered. 'Whoever heard of water on top of a hill!'

Yet when Umbopa climbed up to inspect, the impossible happened. 'Water, water!' he shouted down to us. And there, right in the top of the hill, was Don José's water hole.

With our bellies and our water bottles full, it was now certain that we would reach the mountains – and so in another two days we did.

3 Thirst and hunger

It did not take us long to discover that the desert was not
the only place in which a man might die of thirst or
hunger. The little map told us to climb the 'Left Breast
of Sheba' – the southern of the two peaks. But as we
stood at the stony foot of the great mountain and gazed up
at the snows many thousands of feet above us, we all
wondered how we were to get the strength to climb it.

Our water had gone, and although the white snow above
us promised more water, it was far out of reach. The dried
biltong had all been eaten and hunger was beginning to
gnaw at us. Yet the whole face of the mountain looked
dry and stony. There was no hint there of food or drink
to be had.

But after a short rest we began to climb – and a hard
climb it was. The rock was sharp and jagged, and cut at
our feet. We twisted and turned our way up the steep
slope; but by mid-day the grey wall of the mountain
seemed as high above us as ever. Wearily we staggered
towards a line of boulders to rest for a while.

Then we had the first of two strokes of luck – without
which we should not have survived. When we came over
a ridge we could see that, in a hollow on the mountainside,
a little soil had gathered where grass could grow. And in

31

among the grass were hundreds of small, green water-melons.

We fell on them with a will, and soon the empty rinds of a dozen or more of the moist little fruit lay around us. Once more we were saved from thirst. Then came our second stroke of luck, for as we sat there a great flock of birds came winging over the desert towards us. Ventvögel saw them first – they were bustard, a kind of turkey, and flying high.

'Shoot, master, shoot!' he called to me.

I was flattered by his faith in me, for the shot was impossibly long. Still, I aimed at the flock in a general sort of way and by pure chance brought down a fine, big bird.

You may imagine the feast the five of us made of him! We built a small fire and roasted him, and inside twenty minutes there was only a heap of well-sucked bones left. I am sure I have never tasted better meat.

We rested and went on in much better heart. For a while our adventure began to seem like a pleasure walk. But one bustard is after all only a meal, and we saw no game at all after that. For a day we climbed upward well enough. And for a second day. Yet there was still nothing to eat, and no stream to slake our thirst.

During the third day of our climb we reached the glistening line of snow. At least that solved the problem of our thirst, but it brought with it another danger – that of the cold. We were all weak and underfed. I, for one, was sure that we could not survive a night in the open. Even in the sunshine it was cold enough at this height. At night it would kill us.

There was one hope – and again it was José da Silvestra's map which gave it. In his letter he had written of a small cave near the peak of the mountain. If only we could find it and shelter there, all might be well.

As the evening shadows reached like long fingers across the mountain we walked anxiously, looking for the cave. We seemed to go up and up into the darkness, and still there was no sign. I began to doubt old Don José's word, when suddenly Umbopa stopped and pointed.

'It is the cave,' he said. And there, some two hundred yards away, was a small black hole in the snow.

Thankfully we crept into it out of the night.

I still doubted whether we could survive. The cave was low and black and we had to huddle together to keep warm. Hunger gnawed at us from the inside; cold bit us from the outside. The night seemed to last forever.

I slept little, but sat and listened to the chattering teeth of my companions. Poor Ventvögel, who was next to me, seemed to judder with the cold, and I was sure that he got not a moment's sleep until just before dawn, when he gave a sigh and settled back against me. After that I was able to sleep a little myself, and so at last the wretched night passed.

It was not until the sun rose that we saw the worst of that night's work. As its first light probed into the cave we saw the figure of poor Ventvögel sitting amongst us, stone dead.

With a gasp we drew away from him towards the cave mouth – and then we saw a greater horror. For we had shared our sleep that night not with one dead man, but with two! Sitting hunched but upright in the back of the cave was the parched and dried corpse of a white man!

I do not remember leaving the cave. I know only that suddenly the four of us were sitting dazed on the snow outside.

It was Sir Henry who broke the silence. 'I am going back

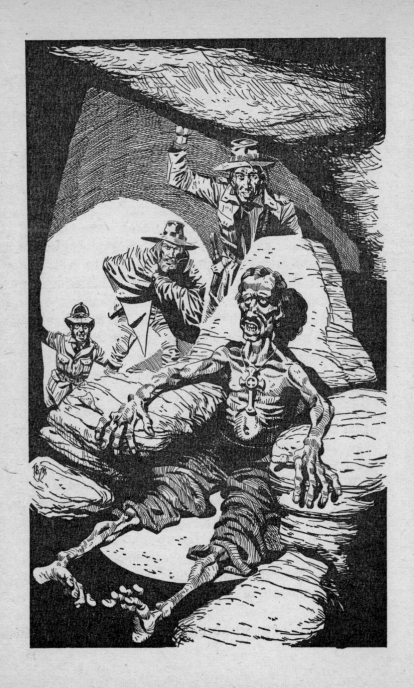

in,' he said, with a shaken but still firm voice.

'Back!' exclaimed Good. 'In heaven's name why?'

'Because,' answered Sir Henry, 'the man in there may be my brother.'

We held our breath as the big man bowed down through the cave entrance again. There was a pause, then a sigh of relief from inside. 'It is not he,' came Sir Henry's voice from inside.

Encouraged by this, we cautiously followed Sir Henry back into the cave.

The unfortunate stranger had been a tall man, dark-haired and with moustachios. His clothes were in tatters, but looked in any case strange.

'Who can it be?' I asked.

'Can't you guess?' answered Good. Sir Henry and I turned to him. 'Why, it is Don José da Silvestra,' he said, simply. 'The clear air and the cold have kept him pretty much as he was when he died – three hundred years ago.'

I cannot imagine a stranger feeling than the one this news gave me. There I sat by the side of a man who had been dead for three hundred years. In my wallet were his last message and map – and there in his hand, I suddenly saw, was the splintered piece of bone he had used as a pen. Strange indeed!

I took the pen, as a memento. Sir Henry took a small crucifix that lay round the dead man's neck. Then we left that bleak, small cave with its two dead men – left them to gaze out over the desert side by side for eternity.

It was soon after we set off again that we crossed the shoulder of the mountain and at last found ourselves heading downwards. A thick morning mist hung over us, but in spite of it we soon saw that the worst of our journey was over. We were coming down into grass-clad rocks. This was the fertile side of the mountain.

Soon we stumbled upon a small herd of mountain deer –
I cannot tell you their name, for I had never seen the
breed before. Three rifle shots rang out, and one of them
brought down a handsome buck. At last we had food
again! It had been almost a week since we had eaten
regularly – and several days since our last meal. I think
we were all ready to eat the little creature whole!

This was just as well, for as we came up to where it lay,
we realised we had no fuel for a fire. There was no help
for it. We should have to eat it raw. It is a strange thing,
but though the idea even now revolts me, I can remember
no finer meat than the meat we ate then. In half an hour
we felt like new men, ready for the next part of our
journey.

'Doesn't Don José mention King Solomon's road on his
map?' asked Sir Henry as we sat there, high on the
mountainside.

I nodded, chewing thoughtfully.

'Then there it is,' he said, and he pointed down to our
right.

The mist had begun to roll back and there, sure
enough, not far below us on the mountain, was the
unmistakeable start of a great road. It must once have led
through a pass in the mountains and out over the desert.
But time had sent rock and sand tumbling over it until
now it finished here.

Quickly we slung on our packs – a little heavier for the
fresh meat we now had – and scrambled down to where
the road began.

And what a road it was! It was a huge, paved highway,
fifty feet wide and dug out of the solid rock. Who knows
what feet of slaves trod on it in olden days! But now our

feet walked lightly along it, glad of the easy passage it gave us.

As we walked we marvelled at the feats of the ancient men who had built it. Here it walked on giant legs across a ravine – there it leaped a river in its bed. No difficulty had been too great for them. Once it even vanished into a tunnel as it cut through a ridge in the mountain. Around the entrance to the tunnel were fine carvings. This surely had been a road for kings, as well as their slaves.

And the land through which we now found ourselves travelling was equally strange and beautiful. What struck me first was that it must be at least five thousand feet higher than the desert on the other side. We had only a little way to come down from the high shoulder of Sheba's Breast. It was a rich and fertile plain that we came down to. Trees grew in lofty clumps. Great grassy hills stretched to the horizon. Swift-flowing rivers cut through them. And over all this lovely landscape, the herds of game roamed free. I think that in all Africa I have never walked in such fine country.

We made good time down Solomon's road, and about mid-day – when the mountains behind us were already growing distant – we paused for a rest. We chose a little glade, shaded by trees and headed by a waterfall, and there we cooked ourselves a second meal.

Afterwards we lay happily back in the grass and watched the scenery. Or at least Sir Henry and Umbopa did. I was too busy watching the odd behaviour of Captain Good.

I may have mentioned that when we set out he insisted on wearing handsome boots, and that he always liked to look smart. Well, after all we had been through he found his appearance most unsatisfactory. I watched as he went down to the little stream and carefully removed his boots,

his trousers and his jacket. Then, sitting in his shirt, he began to dust and brush and clean them as best he could. By the time he was satisfied, and had folded them in a neat pile beside him, I was already greatly amused.

Next he turned his attention to his face, and to my amazement he pulled out a tiny pocket mirror. This he set against a rock. Then, squinting into it, he began to comb his hair. It took him a long time – and even when he had finished he was not satisfied. Gently he felt his chin, on which was a fine growth of beard. Surely, I thought, he is not going to try and shave!

But he was, and did. Slowly and, I should guess by the grunts he made, painfully, he hacked away the bristles down one side of his face. Then he felt the smooth skin with his fingers.

By this time I was almost laughing outright. In fact as he lifted his razor to start the other side of his face I felt sure I must break into laughter. But suddenly, close by the flash of Good's tiny razor, something else flashed through the air. He sprang to his feet, startled, and I saw he was looking at a broad-bladed spear, quivering in the earth beside him.

With my heart pounding I also jumped up – and found myself gazing across the clearing at the tall figures of a group of warriors.

4 Taken by surprise

The Africans, huge copper-coloured men, stood on a little hill above us. One stood with his arm flung out and I guessed it was he who had thrown the spear. He was a youth of about seventeen, and the look on his face was proud and cruel.

All of us had sprung towards our guns once we realised what was happening; and as the group of warriors came down towards us we held them out threateningly. To our surprise this did not impress them at all. Evidently they knew nothing of guns.

At last they stopped and a tall, soldierly old man stepped forward. 'Who are you, strangers – and what do you do in the land of the Kukuanas?' he demanded. To my surprise I found I could understand his language – it was quite close to the Zulu tongue. 'And why,' he went on, 'have three of you white faces, while the fourth is coloured like our mothers' sons?'

It struck me suddenly that he was right. Umbopa was remarkably like them. 'We come in peace, with this man as our servant.'

'You lie!' he said sternly. Then he continued, 'But it does not matter, since you must die any way. It is the king's command that no stranger may live in our land. Prepare to die!'

You may imagine how startled I was at this sudden threat. And even though he could not understand the language, Good evidently gathered what was to be done. As the warriors raised their spears he muttered 'Oh Lord!' and passed his hand across his mouth, flipping down the top set of his false teeth as he did so.

It was a habit he had when alarmed – and this time it was a very fortunate habit indeed. Immediately they saw his teeth move, the Kukuanas ran back a few paces and watched in fear.

I saw our chance. 'Take your teeth out,' I whispered to Good. And with one quick flip of the wrist he had them hidden up his sleeve.

Their leader came nervously forward. 'Why do the teeth of the man with white legs move?' he asked suspiciously. 'And why does he have one shiny eye? And hair on one side of his face but not the other?'

Seeing the advantage we had, Good grinned broadly at them all, showing two pink and toothless gums. Then he swept his hand over his mouth and grinned again. This time there were two rows of pearly teeth.

At this the youth who had tried to spear him threw himself to the ground and began to whimper – and the old gentleman started to grovel.

'Pardon us!' he cried, 'for I see you are spirits and not men at all.'

'You are pardoned,' I said, airily. 'Yes, we are spirits. We come from the highest star that shines by night to see the Kukuana. I have even learned their language!'

'It is so! It is so!' came a chorus of voices.

'Yes,' admitted the old man. 'But you have learned it very badly.'

I silenced him with a look. 'You must be careful that you

do not offend us,' I went on. 'We have ways of dealing with our enemies. Do you see that deer over there?'

A fat buck had appeared on a ridge and it looked as though it was just within rifle-shot. I lifted my gun. I prayed that this time of all times I would not miss. And I brought him down with one clean shot.

This time there was not one of the Kukuanas who did not fall down in fear. The point had been made. And the youth who had thrown at us looked as though he might die of fright.

'Oh, my lords!' said the older man. 'I am Infadoos, uncle of the king – and this is Scragga,' – he pointed to the youth – 'son of Twala, the king. Please do not harm him, or Twala will take my life also.'

'That is true,' said Scragga. And I did not like the voice in which he said it.

'Do not be afraid,' I said. 'We can protect our friends as well as kill our enemies. But take us to this Twala. We must meet your king.'

'Very well, my lords. I will take you to see Twala the king,' said Infadoos.

'Twala the magnificent, Lord of the Kukuanas, Twala the Black, the One-eyed, the Terrible,' put in Scragga. He seemed to enjoy his father's full title. 'But we are hunting three days journey from his palace. Will my lords let us take them there?'

I nodded as graciously as I could, and immediately a group of Kukuanas were signalled to pick up our packs and belongings. The guns, of course, we kept ourselves; but poor Captain Good suddenly found his clothes, including his trousers, being taken up!

'Hey,' he cried in alarm, 'what are they doing with my

trousers? I want them on!' And he made a frantic grab at them.

Infadoos looked round. 'Surely my lord will let his servants carry the things?' he said. He sounded rather hurt!

'But my lord wishes to wear them,' I explained.

Infadoos looked shocked. 'But what have we done that my lord should wish to cover up his beautiful white legs from us?' he asked.

I could see that there was no help for it. For the sake of our story Captain Good would have to look exactly as he did now for the rest of our trip. And when I had explained this to him, the poor man walked off half-clothed and half-shaven – but not at all happy!

Once he had accepted us Infadoos was a pleasant and cheerful guide through his own country. The three day march was pleasantly spent and by careful questioning we learnt much of this strange land.

Of course our first questions were about Sir Henry's brother, George. Had there been any strange white men over the mountains? But even as we asked we suspected there had not. Why else would our faces have seemed so strange to them? Infadoos looked puzzled that we should even ask. No-one had ever crossed the mountains, he assured us.

We hid our disappointment and asked Infadoos about other things, and as the three days went by we learnt much of the land and its customs. Much the most interesting story he told us, however, was that of Twala, the king.

'I am half-brother to Twala, the king,' said Infadoos, when we asked him about himself. 'And half-brother to Imotu, the king that was.'

'How can that be?' I asked, puzzled. Infadoos paused

before he answered, and his face looked pained. Then he began.

'Imotu and Twala, my half-brothers, were twins. Imotu was the elder and stronger – and both were older than I. Now it is the custom of our land that only one of any twins may live. So Twala was given by our father the king to Gagool, the witch, to kill.'

I started at the mention of this name. Surely it was the name old Don José had mentioned! But I did not interrupt, and Infadoos went on.

'But Gagool did not kill Twala, and many years later, when Imotu was king, she brought out his twin. She was clever. She waited for a time when Imotu was sick of a hunting wound. Then she gathered the people before his hut and cried to them that he was not their king. "This is your true king!" she told them, pointing to Twala. And then all the people believed her, because around Twala's loins was the tattoo of the royal snake. Only the king can wear it.

'Then the people cried out, "Koom! Koom!" That is the salute we give our kings. And Imotu came out of his hut with his wife and his baby son, Ignosi. But he was weak with his wound and Twala laughed at him and killed him with his spear. His wife took Ignosi, the child, and fled with him to the mountains. There they must have died. And since then Twala has been king amongst us. He and Gagool rule us.'

It was a sad story – and rather frightening. What we had heard of Twala so far did not make any of us confident that he would welcome us. But we had little more time to worry about this, for our journey was nearly over. In the afternoon of the third day we came in sight of the Kraal where the king's palace lay. It was a fine, wide circle of gleaming white huts, protected from outside by a deep ditch. In the middle towered up a very much larger hut, with a large open space around it. Clearly this was the palace of Twala the king.

Infadoos, seeing that we were gazing down, came over. 'That is Loos,' he said, 'our chief town.' He sounded proud of it.

'But why,' asked Sir Henry, 'does the road not lead to it?'

We looked, and it was true. The road passed a few miles to the north and ran on into the distance.

'The road ends there, at the mountains we call the Three Witches,' answered Infadoos. And he pointed at the far horizon. We shaded our eyes and looked. There they were. Not round and massive, like Sheba's Breasts, but steep, jagged, wicked-looking mountains.

'But why should the road end there?' I asked.

Infadoos looked suddenly suspicious. 'Who knows?' he said. 'There are only caves there – caves and the Place of Death where we bury our kings.'

'But I have heard that there are heaps of shining pebbles and metal that gleams like the morning sun,' I said.

'My lord from the stars should know these things better than I,' answered Infadoos. 'If you would find out more, you must ask Gagool.'

I could see that it would not do to question him further. He seemed very touchy on the subject. All the same I could not help turning to Sir Henry when he had gone.

'Those are King Solomon's Mines! You can be sure of it,' I whispered. I could hardly contain my excitement.

'Yes, those are the mines. And since the white man likes to play with such rocks and pebbles, you shall have them.'

The voice came softly from behind us. It was Umbopa again!

This time he said no more, but turned and walked away. Sir Henry frowned. 'That fellow knows a lot more than he is saying,' he commented.

Good and I agreed – but there was nothing we could do. All the same we none of us felt as safe as we should have liked as we came into Loos. Infadoos, who had seemed friendly enough, now seemed distant and cold. Scragga did not look as if he liked us at all. And now Umbopa was again behaving mysteriously.

We were thankful to be taken straight to an airy and pleasant hut where we were to spend the night in peace before meeting Twala in the morning.

5 The king

We were wakened early and told that Twala would see us
in an hour's time. Already the Kraal seemed alive with
preparations for the great event – and we decided we must
look the part of 'men from the stars'. We cleaned and
tidied ourselves as best we could. Poor Good even shaved
the one half of his face again, but we would not let him
touch the other! We did ask Infadoos if he could have
his trousers back. The answer was no. Apparently they
had been sent to the king as holy relics!

At last the moment arrived. We were led out from our
hut into the open space around the king's palace, and
there we waited. All of us fingered our rifles nervously.

Drawn up in perfect ranks around us were row upon row
of the most magnificent warriors I have ever seen. Grey
ostrich plumes hung from their heads across their broad,
coppery shoulders. Each man carried a long shield on his
left arm and a broad-bladed spear, like an assegai, in his
right hand. Not one of them was less than six feet tall,
and not one stirred a muscle.

There was a hush so deep that you would never have
known there was a soul there. Everyone was waiting for
the king. Then at last he came. Out of the palace strode an
enormous figure. Truly, even amongst these people he
seemed a giant. The boy, Scragga, who walked beside

him, was tiny by comparison. Perhaps only Sir Henry matched him for height.

The king stepped forward and stood, glowering at us with a proud and cruel look. We saw that he had indeed only one eye – and we saw also why Scragga had called him 'the Terrible'.

Still no-one moved. There was no sound.

Then from behind Twala a little monkey-like creature scuttled out, and from it came a high, thin voice. 'Be humble, oh people!' it cried. 'It is the king!'

At once the silence was broken by thousands of voices giving back the cry – 'It is the king! It is the king!'

Then there was silence again. But only for a moment. Someone, among the ranks of soldiers, dropped a shield and it fell with a clatter to the ground.

Twala turned his one eye in the direction of the noise and bellowed, 'Who is the son of a dog who shames his king? Step out the man that dropped his shield.'

There was a pause. Then a handsome young man stepped forward a few paces. His face was pale. He looked at Twala and said, nervously, 'It was an accident, oh king.'

'Then it is an accident you must pay for,' said Twala. 'You have made your king foolish in the eyes of his visitors. Prepare to die!'

We had scarcely time to realise what was happening before it was done. At a nod from his father, Scragga stepped forward and twirled his spear. The young man did nothing, but covered his eyes with his hands. Then there was a flash of steel, and the spear blade was sticking out between the poor unfortunate's shoulders.

At once, Sir Henry was on his feet. 'But it's murder! Cold-blooded murder!' he said, outraged. He was already reaching for his rifle when I pulled him back.

'For God's sake, man, sit still! We can do nothing – and if you try we will all be killed.' I could see Twala looking at us, and I was glad when Sir Henry managed to overcome his anger and sit down.

'Greetings, strangers in my land,' said the king.

'Greetings,' I replied – though we none of us felt very welcome.

Suddenly he pointed to the body of the youth, who was being dragged away. 'Tell me,' he asked, 'why should I not make you all like him?'

I laughed. I must admit I did not feel very brave – but I laughed. 'Why, king,' I said, 'have they not told you that we come from the stars and that we can kill from afar?'

'They have told me – but I, Twala, do not believe. Kill me a man – one of those, over there – and I will believe.'

I shook my head. 'No, king. I will kill you an animal – but we do not kill men unless they have deserved to die. Drive in an ox.'

But Twala was not to be put off. 'Unless you kill me a man, I shall not believe that you can,' he said, stubbornly.

It was a tricky position. We had to impress the king, but none of us would shoot one of his innocent people.

Then I had an idea. 'Very well, king,' I said. 'If you yourself will walk across the clearing, I promise you you will not reach the gate alive. Or let Scragga stand forward to be killed.'

Truly, nothing would have given me greater pleasure than to shoot that young man! But the idea did not appeal to him, for he gave a cry of fear and ran back inside the palace.

Twala scowled, but admitted defeat. 'Drive in an ox!' he called. And soon a wretched, scraggy beast stood at the far end of the clearing. This time I made Sir Henry do the shooting, so that they would know we could all kill. He was a bit nervous, but fortunately our luck held. With one shot he put a bullet through the animal's heart, and as it fell a murmur of amazement ran round. Even Twala looked impressed.

But before Twala could speak again, there was a strange interruption. The little, monkey-like creature that had spoken earlier scuttled in front of the king and stood up. Only then did we realise that it was a woman – but what a strange woman!

Age had shrunk her to the size of a child. Age greater than one can imagine had shrivelled and dried her skin so that it hung loosely round her in folds. Her eyes had sunk back into her skull – but they gazed fiercely at us from within their caves. And with one bony, scratchy finger she pointed at us. Then she spoke.

'Listen, oh king! Listen, oh people of the Kukuanas! Let all things living that must die, and all things dead that must live again, hear the words of Gagool! I prophesy!'

Her words died away in a thin wail, and terror seemed to seize on all of us. She was very terrible.

Then she started to speak again in a sing-song voice.

'Blood! Blood! Rivers of blood! I smell – I taste the strong, salt taste of blood!

'Footsteps! Footsteps! Shaking the mountains! I hear the footsteps of the white man!

'Who made the stone on your forehead, king? Who made the coat of mail that you wear?'

Twala fingered the bright diamond on his brow and ran his hand over his shirt of fine mail. He looked as fearful as we.

'You do not know – but I know,' went on Gagool. 'It was

the white men who came before you, and who will come after you.'

She turned to us. 'You come looking for the bright pebbles. But will you go away with them, or will you stay with me? Will the blood dry on the earth?' Then she swung round to face Umbopa. 'And you, what do you seek? It cannot be the stones. I think I know – I think I see – Strip off the girdle . . .'

Gagool, whose voice had risen higher and higher as she looked at Umbopa, now broke off and fell to the ground.

It was as though a terrible spell had been broken.

Twala had the twitching little body carried out, and turned to face us. 'White people from the stars,' he said, 'you have heard the words of Gagool. It is in my mind that I must kill you.'

Again I laughed, and raised my rifle. 'Do you think we would let you?' I asked him.

He seemed to think for a moment. Then he said, 'Go in peace. Tonight is the night of the great dance. You shall see it and be safe. Tomorrow I will think.'

And with that we were led back to our hut.

Infadoos was about to leave us at the door when I beckoned him to come in. 'Your king is a cruel man,' I said as he sat down.

Infadoos sighed. 'He is. Men die every day, either for no reason or because Twala wants their lands. The whole land of the Kukuanas groans under his rule.'

'Then why do you sit quietly and allow it to happen? Why do some of you not rise against Twala and kill him?' I asked.

Infadoos shook his head. 'He is the king. And even if we did kill him, Scragga would reign in his place. His heart is blacker than his father's!' The old man looked helpless.

'If only Imotu were still king – or if his son, Ignosi, had survived. But they are both dead!'

'How do you know that Ignosi is dead?' Umbopa's deep, quiet voice came from behind us.

Infadoos turned impatiently on him. 'Be silent, boy! What do you know of Ignosi?'

But Umbopa would not be silent. 'Listen,' he went on mysteriously, 'and I will tell you a story. You know that when king Imotu was killed his wife took the baby Ignosi up into the mountains. Now I tell you that they did not die there. They went down into the desert, where a tribe of wandering desert men found them. Then they travelled far and the boy Ignosi was brought up in a distant land. His mother died, but before she died she told him this. Many years passed, and then the man Ignosi heard that a party of white men intended to cross the desert to his home. And so he came back to the land where Imotu his father was king.'

We listened to this in amazement – and I could see that Infadoos was growing angry. But before he could say anything, Umbopa stood up. He slipped off the linen girdle he wore and towered naked over us.

'Behold Ignosi, king of the Kukuanas!' he cried in a great voice.

All around his waist ran the tattoo of a blue snake – the mark of the king.

Infadoos fell to his knees. 'Koom! Koom!' he cried. 'The king has come back!'

6 Death dance

When we had recovered from the surprise, we began to look at our situation in a new light. Umbopa – or Ignosi as I must now call him – had come back to claim his crown. But it did not seem likely that Twala would give it him! Nor could he count on all the Kukuanas believing right away that he was the king.

Of course Sir Henry offered him his support, and so did Captain Good once he had promised him his trousers back. Speaking for myself I am not very fond of revolutions and battles. But since Umbopa had stuck by us, I felt I ought to stick by him – so I promised my help, too, in return for some of those diamonds!

Infadoos then told us that after the great dance he would sound out a few men he could trust, and perhaps in that way he could get Ignosi some support. 'If,' he went on, 'we are all still alive after the dancing.'

These were most alarming words. But we had no time to ask more, for just then a messenger came in from Twala. He brought us gifts. Three chain-mail shirts like the one Twala had worn, and three battle-axes.

The shirts were amazingly light and thin – but strong. Infadoos told us, as we put them on, that they had been made hundreds of years ago. 'There are only a few left,' he said. 'Either the king is well pleased or very afraid of you – or he would not have sent them.'

Then we buckled on our revolvers and went out to the dance.

Once more we came to the open space before the king's palace. Again it was full of men – tall soldiers like the one we had seen killed earlier. It was dark now, and the light from many fires glinted on the spears of at least twenty thousand men.

All waited without making a sound.

'Why are they so silent?' I whispered to our guide.

He looked grimly at me. 'Those in danger of death do not laugh and chatter,' he said.

I wondered what kind of dance it was to be.

Twala the king began it. For a while he stood still in front of his silent people, with Gagool behind him. Then he raised his spear and the feet of twenty thousand men struck the ground together. The earth seemed to shake. Again he lifted his spear, and again they stamped. And again, and again, until they were pounding a steady rhythm. Then the singing began.

I cannot begin to describe the strange beauty of that chant and dance. It rose, it fell, wavering on in long-drawn notes. It swelled like a wave of the sea. And it sank at last into silence again.

Then suddenly the mood changed. In among the silent warriors dashed ten strange figures. They were women, old women – though not so old as Gagool – and round their waists hung circlets of human bones. Together they rushed through the ranks of soldiers and stood at last in front of the king.

Then Gagool came forward.

'Are you ready, my daughters?' she croaked.

'We are ready, we are ready, oh mother!'

'Will you find the man who has thought evil of the king?'

'We will find him, we will find him!'

'Then begin!' shrieked Gagool.

We watched, fascinated, as they rushed back towards the men. At first we could not see what they meant to do. But we did not have to wait long. One of the creatures was creeping towards a line of men just by us. The men looked afraid. Then suddenly she stopped by a tall, grey-headed warrior, and pointed at him with a bone.

'I smell him! The enemy of the king!'

At once the poor man was seized by his companions and dragged out to Twala. He did not struggle – indeed from the limp way his feet dragged he did not seem conscious.

'Kill!' said Twala. And 'Kill!', 'Kill!' echoed Scragga and Gagool. At once a soldier passed his broad assegai through the man's body, while another dashed out his brains with a club. Then the lifeless form was thrown to one side. Before it had landed, another was on top of it, and another. Horrified, I turned to Infadoos. 'How many will die tonight?' I asked him.

'Very many,' he answered, simply. And his face was grey.

It was a night of horror. Slowly the pile of bodies mounted until there must have been more than a hundred. But the people stood in silence and did nothing – even though they all knew they might die. It seemed that they were fascinated by their fear of the witches. And of Twala.

Even we stood silent among them – until the inevitable happened. The ten witches were no longer picking victims, but the witch-mother, Gagool, was now picking hers! Round and round she danced, crooning to herself. It seemed as though she was looking for someone special.

It was Sir Henry who first realised that she was coming

to us. His hand tightened on the revolver at his side and he whispered to me, 'Which one of us is it to be?'

Nearer and nearer danced the evil little creature. Then suddenly the bone in her hand was pointing straight out in front of her – at Umbopa, the newly-found Ignosi!

There was a moment of shock and surprise. Ignosi gripped his spear and looked as though he would fight for his life. But in the silence that followed his choosing I called out to Twala, 'But you cannot kill your guest! Spare him!'

Twala scowled. 'Gagool has smelled him out. He brings evil to the king. He must die!'

Three warriors, red with blood, moved towards him. But we had promised him our help and we were not going to let him down. I pointed my revolver straight at Twala, while Sir Henry and Good drew theirs.

'If your men try to take Umbopa, you will die,' I said to Twala. 'Remember the ox!'

Twala was shaken – and I could see rage in Gagool's face. At last the king spoke. 'I spare him. Not because I am afraid, but because he is a guest. Go! Take him. The dance is finished!'

'That,' I said as we walked back again to our hut, 'was horrible.'

Sir Henry nodded, and Captain Good said angrily, 'The man is a monster! Just say the word, Umbopa, when you want to start your revolution – and I'm your man!'

'That depends on how far my uncle has succeeded in his plans,' said Umbopa. And that reminded us that Infadoos had hoped to bring men, leaders of their people, to our hut after the dance.

We had not long to wait. Shortly after midnight Infadoos and twelve dignified chiefs slipped quietly in and

sat in a circle on the floor. We listened as Infadoos told
our story again – and then as Ignosi stripped off his girdle
and told his part of the story. All this was done in
whispers, and we waited anxiously to see how the chiefs
would take it.

They talked together for a while after Ignosi had finished. Then they turned to us. 'My lords,' said one, 'a man may have a snake tattooed upon him easily enough. How shall we truly know that this is Ignosi? Give us a sign!'

They did not believe. We could not blame them, since they were being asked to go to war on our side. But it was desperately disappointing – and we had no sign.

Then Good seemed to have an idea. He got out a small diary and flipped through the pages in some excitement. Then he turned to the chiefs.

'So you fellows want a sign,' he said. 'Then you shall have one. Look outside and tell me what you see.'

The chiefs did so. 'Only the moon,' said one, puzzled.

'Then tell me,' went on Good, 'can any mortal man put out the moon?' They shook their heads and looked suspiciously at the Captain. 'Very well,' he said, cheerfully, 'tomorrow night, about two hours before midnight, we will put out the moon – and then perhaps you will believe all that we tell you.'

'If my lords can do this thing, then truly we will believe,' answered the chief. But he looked as though he had as little idea as I had how we were going to do it!

Then silently they filed out and left us. Instantly we turned to Good with our questions. How were we to do this magic? And what would happen when we failed – as surely we must?

The Captain silenced us by handing us his diary. There, against the date 4th June, was the following printed notice: 'Total eclipse of the moon, begins 8.15 pm. Visible throughout Europe and Africa.'

'And,' said Good triumphantly, 'I calculate that at 8.15 in England it will be about 10.00 here!'

'Well,' said Sir Henry, 'I hope this information is correct.'

And so did we all, for on it now hung all our success.

The following day was an anxious one for us, and as evening drew near we became quite nervous. This was not helped by the arrival of Twala's messenger. Once again we were summoned – not this time to a men's dance, but to the dance of the girls.

The previous evening had given us more than enough of the Kukuanas' dances, and it was with some alarm that we accepted the king's invitation. But tonight he seemed in a good humour. We were seated by him and treated to the most lovely dance of maidens. Each girl carried a palm leaf and a lily, and all were young and beautiful. They moved in a steady pattern, and I could not help noticing one girl in particular. Her dancing drew everyone's eyes.

At the end of the dance, Twala turned to me and said, 'They are lovely, are they not? Which do you think is the fairest?'

Before I had thought I pointed to the girl who had drawn my attention. Twala nodded in satisfaction. 'I think so too,' he said. 'So she will be the sacrifice.'

I looked at him in horror. Surely he could not be intending to kill the lovely creature who had danced so beautifully? But yes – there was the hated Scragga again sharpening his spear. And the look of fear on the girl's face told me it was so.

Now, I am not a man to risk his life carelessly, but I am certain I would have done something to help the poor girl. As things turned out, though, I did not need to. Captain Good was a gentleman in more than the way he dressed. Seeing what was to happen he jumped down and stood at her side. 'Don't worry,' he said cheerily. 'We'll look after you.' And before we knew what was happening he had brought her to us.

As he did so Scragga came towards us with his spear level. He clearly intended to kill his sacrifice in spite of us. I looked at my watch. Only a few minutes to ten! We desperately needed the eclipse now – but the moon was as bright as ever.

Something had to be done. Quickly I stepped forward in front of the girl and turned to Twala. 'King, this is enough! You must not kill the girl. Let her go!' I tried to sound more confident than I felt.

But my words did not help. 'Must not!' bellowed Twala in a rage. 'Who are you to tell the king that he must not? Scragga, kill the girl! Guards, seize these men!'

At once a dozen burly warriors stepped towards us. We levelled our rifles, but it looked hopeless. In despair I stepped forward again. 'Stop!' I called – and to my amazement they did. 'You are mad, king, if you think you can threaten us. Call off your soldiers and let the girl go. If you do not we will put out the moon and cover the land in darkness.'

It was a rash threat. Everything now hung on the eclipse – and it had not yet begun. Gagool seemed to think so too. 'Let them do it,' she called out, 'or let them die with the girl! No man may put out the moon!'

I looked up in despair. And at last, there was the thin, dark line clipping the edge of the bright moon! I lifted my hand and pointed. Sir Henry and the Captain pointed too. And as the people saw what was happening, a terrible fear seemed to come over them. Some fell down and wept. Some ran. The chiefs we had spoken to already came to us and bowed to Ignosi. But fear gripped them all as the blackness crept across the land.

Suddenly Scragga, who had stood all this time with his spear poised, shrieked out in terror. 'They have murdered the moon! The white men have murdered the moon! Kill them!' And he hurled his spear full at Sir Henry's broad chest.

The chain mail which we all wore under our clothes was marvellously strong. Even though the blow staggered him, Sir Henry was unharmed. The spear fell at his feet and at once he seized it. With one thrust he sent it straight through Scragga, and the king's son lay dead.

A cry of horror came from Twala and his people and, as the darkness at last covered the land, they fled.

7 Hill battle

All day we had worked hard to fortify the hill, and now we could look down on the king's palace at Loos confident that we could face his attack.

Some twenty thousand men had come over to Ignosi after the eclipse and we had set up our camp on a high, flat-topped hill overlooking the Kraal. We knew that Twala had perhaps twice as many men still with him, but we had with us the crack regiment of his army, the Greys. And those who fought alongside us were fighting for freedom.

I sat by Sir Henry and the Captain as Ignosi spoke to his troops. 'Do you know,' I said to Sir Henry, 'I am just beginning to realise what we have let ourselves in for – and I must admit I am scared.'

Sir Henry looked at me oddly. 'You often say things like that,' he commented. 'And I can never quite believe you. Still,' he went on, 'you are right. There are going to be many killed in this battle, and I suppose we will have to be in the thick of it. We've a reputation to keep up.'

He was trying to sound as though he would rather not have to fight. But I think he was looking forward to it.

He did not have long to wait. 'Macumazahn!' called Ignosi to me. 'They are coming!'

We crossed over to the edge of the hill. At once we could see the huge column of Twala's troops coming out of Loos.

'It looks bad,' I said. 'They are dividing up. I think they are going to attack in three directions at once.'

'Then we must be ready for them,' said Sir Henry. And he strode off down the hill to the outer line of defence. He intended to be among the first to meet the enemy.

I watched him go and thought again what a magnificent figure he cut. As well as the chain mail, he had found himself a feathered crest, a battle-axe, and a small round shield. With his flowing blond hair and beard he looked like some old Viking chief!

I waited behind the third line of defence and we watched as Twala's men drew nearer. My skill was with a rifle, not a battle-axe, and as they came within range I tried to pick off their officers. Every time a man fell a great cheer rose from our regiments. But still Twala's men came on.

Then with a roar they were on us.

Our men stood stoutly at their posts, but Twala's army

was huge. Soon our outer line of defence had retreated to join the second – and that, too, was being pushed steadily back up hill. The slaughter was terrible. The broad assegais opened up gaping wounds and blood drenched the ground.

Now Twala's men had come up to our last line and things looked bad for us. Back and forth swayed the two masses of struggling men. Then suddenly I saw Sir Henry's huge form surge downhill into the opposing army. At once they began to give ground in front of him. I watched as he swung down on warrior after warrior. No-one could stand before him. Slowly Twala's men were being pushed back.

Then a cry from behind me told me that things were not going so well over there. Up that side of the hill our men had been pushed right back and the enemy had nearly broken through.

At once Ignosi called on all of us at the top of the hill to follow him. And since there was no help for it I joined the charge. I remember a clash of shields as the two forces met, and I also remember following close to Ignosi, who cut down all who stood in his path. Then, suddenly, there was a huge man, with a spear in his hand and a snarl on his face, charging straight at me!

I must admit I am quite proud of my presence of mind. I immediately fell flat on the ground so that the big man stumbled right across me. Then I got up and shot him.

But that is all I do remember, for at once I felt a blow on the back of my head. I took no further part in the fighting . . .

I woke up to Sir Henry's grave face peering into my own. 'Thank heavens!' he said. 'We were afraid you were badly hurt.'

'Not I,' I said. I sat up and rubbed my head. 'But how do things stand with us?'

'Well – and not so well,' he answered. 'We have driven them off, but now they are camping at the foot of the hill. We are besieged, I am afraid. And we have no water up here.'

Ignosi, who was by him, joined in. 'Aye,' he said. 'We have won one battle, but lost many men. And we still have not won the war. Whatever we do next will decide whether we are to win or lose. Therefore I would hear what Macumazahn has to say before I decide. He is cunning, like the fox.'

I thought for a moment. Being a cautious man I was not for attacking straight away. Yet we had many wounded, I could see. And by tomorrow they would be worse, not better. 'Twala will not expect us to attack him,' I said. 'And the longer we sit up here, the worse for us. So it seems to me that since we must attack him, the sooner we do so the better.'

'That's it!' growled Sir Henry. 'Let's get at them again!'

'So the fox and the lion agree,' said Ignosi. 'And I agree with them. I have made up my mind to strike again at Twala my uncle today. Listen. Here is what we must do.'

We listened as Ignosi unfolded to us his master plan. And I think we all knew as we listened that not only the future of the Kukuanas depended on it, but our own lives also.

It seemed that we had lost some two thousand men during the day. Twala, on the other hand, had been receiving new regiments, and must now outnumber us two to one – or even more. The plan was that we must meet Twala in a narrow ravine on the mountainside, where all his forces could not be used at once. And the men chosen for the task of holding the ravine against the might of Twala's army were Infadoos's famous regiment, the Greys.

Ignosi would wait in reserve and would charge only when the rest of his army had reached their positions. They were to divide into two and come down on either side of Twala's forces. But it was obvious to us all that the last part of the plan would be pointless if the Greys had not already managed to break the back of Twala's attack.

When Ignosi had finished speaking he turned to us. 'In the fighting I would have Macumazahn by my side, for he is wise. But will my friend Incubu fight in the front rank of the Greys?' He looked firmly at Sir Henry as he spoke. 'It will strike fear into the heart of Twala to see your broad axe swinging at his warriors.'

So, I thought, this is how the expedition is to end. We shall find neither George Curtis nor the diamonds, but will end on a battlefield, each with a spear between his shoulders. While I was lost in my own thoughts, Infadoos was quietly telling his Greys what they were to do. They were none of them young – all seasoned veterans. I marvelled at the calm dignity with which they heard his news. With them was Sir Henry, and even he looked grim-faced. They all knew they were being asked to make their last stand.

When Infadoos had finished speaking his men turned to Ignosi. With their spear-hafts they slowly began to beat on their shields. Slowly the noise they made grew and grew, till it was like the sound of a great war drum booming. They were saluting their king.

Then they wheeled about and marched in perfect order down the mountain to their position. At once we could see that Twala had noticed. Within minutes lines of warriors started to stream across the plain towards the point of the hill where Infadoos's men were coming down. They seemed as many as the sands of the sea. And when the Greys reached the narrowest point of the ravine and arranged themselves in three lines across it, they seemed

very few indeed. Then we waited as the cries of Twala's warriors grew louder.

We had not long to wait. Round the corner of the ravine came the first regiment of Twala's army. And stopped. We could see messengers running back and forth, and

Twala himself, furious that he could not send his whole army out at once and crush us.

Then the first regiment came on alone. Like a wave on the sea shore they reared up and up towards Infadoos's silent men. Then they crashed down upon them and the Greys seemed buried under their weight.

We waited, half in fear and half in hope, while the bloody hand-to-hand fighting went on. Then, amazingly, the numbers of Twala's regiment seemed to dwindle. The great wave trickled back into the sand. And the Greys stood steady and alone again. They had destroyed an entire regiment!

But we did not cheer. Only two of their three lines remained – and a fresh regiment now faced them.

Imagine our horror at having to stand back and watch as regiment after regiment was hurled against our best men. Each one took a little longer to fall. After each, there were fewer and fewer Greys left to oppose them. Occasionally I caught sight of Sir Henry's massive form, brushing warriors aside like flies. At least he was still alive. But I could not bear to be idle when my friend was in the thick of the fight.

'Are we going to stand here all day?' I asked Ignosi.

'No,' was his answer. 'See, the trap is ready and the Greys have done their work!' Then he lifted up his great war-spear and shouted his battle cry.

It is beyond me to describe what happened next. I was borne along in a hurrying sea of men. I remember the shouts and the screams. I also remember seeing Sir Henry and Twala somewhere quite close to me. Like giants they met in the middle of the battle, swung at each other and were swept apart by the struggling masses of their comrades.

I could not have said whether we were winning or losing. But suddenly, from above us, to right and left, came the wild cries of our comrades. Twala's men looked up, and you could see the dismay on their faces! For down the hillside and onto them from either side swept the last third of our army! It was soon over. The shock of the final attack swept the shattered remains of Twala's once great army down the ravine and out onto the plain below.

And then a kind of quietness came on the hillside. For of the three thousand men who had stood with Infadoos against Twala's regiments, only ninety-five remained. Truly they had broken the back of Twala's army. But it had been a terrible last stand for the Greys.

Mercifully Sir Henry was unharmed. The chain mail

had served him well. But when we set off in search of Good, we came upon a less pleasant sight. He had been part of the last charge from the side, and so had pursued Twala's running men further down the hill. Good was sitting by the path, near the body of a Kukuana. Suddenly, and before we could warn our friend, the 'body' sprang to its feet, knocked down the Captain and began to spear him savagely!

By the time we reached him, he lay unconscious, and although his chain mail had saved him from death, he was obviously badly hurt.

So it was that when we entered the king's palace at Loos with Ignosi, we felt a mixture of feelings. Triumph at the victory, but grief at our friend's injury.

The sight that met us there, though, added another feeling – disgust. For sitting calmly in the middle of the courtyard was Twala. And by him sat Gagool.

As we came nearer, Twala stood, and fixed the gaze of his one eye on Ignosi. Even then, we were aware of what a huge and powerful man he was.

'Hail, oh king!' he called bitterly. 'Tell me, you who were a guest in my land, what fate have you for me?'

Ignosi returned his gaze steadily. 'The same that you gave my father, Twala,' he said. 'Death!'

'Then at least let me die by the custom of my people – in single fight with one enemy.'

Ignosi hesitated. Then, 'It is granted,' he said. 'Who would you fight?'

The custom was that a condemned man could challenge any man to fight him – and keep on challenging until he was killed. Suddenly the horrible thought occurred that he might choose me!

But no. His gaze was fixed on Sir Henry! 'I will fight

Incubu,' he said. 'Unless he is afraid!'

I think that Ignosi would have stopped it if it had not been for that last taunt. But once he had been accused of cowardice, nothing would stop Sir Henry – tired though he was – from accepting the challenge.

I feared for my friend. Twala was as big a man as he, and was fighting for his life. But a clearing was made and into it stepped the two men. Each bore a battle-axe and a knife, with a shield on the left arm.

At a sign from Ignosi they began.

At first they circled each other carefully, swinging out with their axes. One or two blows rang on shields, but nothing struck home until Sir Henry leapt forward and slashed down at Twala, gashing him in the shoulder. The blow seemed to madden the old king, for at once he unleashed a terrible swing at Sir Henry. The axe cut clean through, shattering the axe-handle. His shield was split, and a great wound appeared down the side of his face.

We gasped in horror to see him wounded and defenceless. But he quickly sprang at Twala and seized him around the waist. Now each man struggled to break the other's grip. Sinews strained and cracked under

those bear-hugging arms. And all the time Twala struck as best he could with his axe.

At last Sir Henry seemed to realise that without the axe he was lost. Letting the king go, he suddenly plucked the axe from him and sprang back. At once Twala had his knife out and made a violent lunge at Sir Henry. The blow struck him full on the breast – but again the mail did its work.

Then the broad blade of the axe swung once – and Twala's head seemed to bound from his shoulders.

Twala the king, the one-eyed, the terrible, was dead. I stepped forward and lifted the great diamond from his forehead, where it lay in the dust and blood. Then I bound it on Ignosi's brow.

'Hail, Ignosi, king of the Kukuanas!' I cried.

And back came the answer, 'Koom! Koom! Ignosi!'

8 The mines at last

The night was a strange one. Two of my comrades were hurt, and even though I was uninjured I found it hard to sleep. Every time I shut my eyes my head was full of whirling warriors – and when I lay awake the silence of the night was broken by the wails of women for their dead menfolk.

We were given Twala's own bedchamber to rest in. So it happened that after we had roughly stitched up his wound, Sir Henry slept on the bed of the man he had just killed. Though the wound would scar him for life, it was not dangerous.

Not so with poor Good. He was badly bruised and had lost a lot of blood from a wound in one of his famous white legs. By morning it was clear that his condition was bad. A fever had set in.

The days that followed were anxious ones. As Sir Henry recovered, Good seemed to weaken. While we walked around the Kraal taking the air, he lay inside, tossing on a sick-bed. But he was not alone, and I believe it was thanks to his companion that his life was saved.

You will remember that it was Good who had insisted on saving the life of that beautiful dancer, the night of the eclipse. She had not forgotten him. Foulata was her name, and except when she was preparing some nourishing soup for him, she never left the Captain's side. For a week she tended him, while we came and went and worried. I do not remember that she ever slept.

Then one evening I came into the bedchamber and found everything unusually still and quiet. The Captain had moaned and threshed his way through the fever, so it was odd to come into a silent room. My first and awful thought was that he was dead. I turned to Foulata, the question on my lips. But she smiled and signalled me to be silent.

With relief I saw that he was sleeping peacefully. The fever had broken, and his recovery was certain.

The days that followed were sweet indeed. We were treated royally by the Kukuanas, who had all now gladly accepted their new king. And as the days passed, strength came back to Captain Good. He could now walk, aided by Foulata – who seemed wholly devoted to him.

Of Ignosi we saw little. He was busy ordering his affairs. But there was one matter that I had not forgotten and which I was determined to raise with him. I had his promise that the treasures of King Solomon's Mines should be ours – if their secret could be found.

When at last the king seemed to have time to talk, I raised with him the matter of that secret. He had happened to remark that Gagool, not Twala, had been the evil of the land.

'What do you mean to do with her, then?' I asked.

His face darkened. 'She must die,' he said firmly. 'Then that evil will die with her.'

'True,' I said. 'But then her knowledge will die with her. Perhaps she knows where the treasure of the Mines lies hidden?'

Ignosi looked at me. 'I had forgotten, Macumazahn,' he

said. 'Perhaps it may be that Gagool does know. If she will show you where it is, she shall live. Let her be brought to me.'

Soon the wizened little figure stood before us, spitting curses at all of us. 'Have a care, Gagool,' warned Ignosi. 'It is in my mind to kill you!'

The threat seemed to throw her into a rage. 'You!

Kill me? It is not possible. Do you know – do any of you know how old Gagool is? Of course you do not! For I was old before the oldest of you were young. And you speak of killing Gagool! I tell you that no man may kill Gagool. Only chance can end her life!'

'All the same I will kill you,' said Ignosi as though she had never spoken, 'if you do not tell what you know of the secret of the caves at the end of the Great Road.'

For the first time in her life it seemed to occur to Gagool that her life was in danger. At once her face became cunning. 'At the end of the Great Road?' she said. 'Why, who does not know what lies there? First there is the road. Then there are the Silent Ones – the three stone watchers. Then there is the pit. And there lies the Place of Death, where even now Twala sits with his ancestors.'

She fell silent. 'And beyond that, Gagool? What lies beyond?' Ignosi had risen to his feet and stood over the wretched little creature.

Suddenly she spat at him. 'Beyond that lies what only I, Gagool, know! And you will never know. None of you! It is my secret and I carry it with me.'

'Then you will carry it to your grave,' said Ignosi. And slowly he began to bring his spear down on her.

Nearer it came, and nearer. She fell down, a pathetic heap of old rags. Then she shrieked, 'You dare not! No man dare kill Gagool! You will be accursed forever!'

Ignosi's hand never faltered. Down came the blade until its sharp point touched her neck. In another moment, I knew, Gagool would be dead. And with her would go her secret.

Then, at the very moment when the sharp point pricked her, she sprang away, crying: 'Nay, I will show them! I will take them to the treasure house! Only let me live to sit in the sun a little longer.'

Ignosi withdrew his spear. 'Do you swear this, witch?' he asked.

'Gagool does not break her word. The white men shall see the King's Treasure.'

So it came about that several days later we found ourselves under the towering cliffs of the Three Witches. The road led straight to their foot and Gagool had seemed almost pleased to be taking us there. In a valley between these craggy peaks lay a deep pit, and over it stood the three statues Gagool had called the Silent Ones.

They were immense. Two male figures and one female sat on the very brink of the pit, towering twenty feet over our heads. It was as if they had been set there in ancient days to guard that pit. And when I looked at it closely, I knew why it needed a guard!

It had been dug out to a great depth – some three hundred feet, I would guess. And its sides sloped steeply down. It would have been a walk of perhaps half a mile to go round it – and beyond all question it was a diamond mine.

Infadoos, who was our guard and our guide, came up as we gazed at the wonders around us. 'Will my lords enter the Place of Death now, or will they eat first? Gagool is ready to be your guide. I can take you no further.'

All of us had waited too long, been through too much, travelled too far, to be patient now. At once I had Foulata fill a basket with such food as we might need for a meal later. Then we were led by Gagool to the small, black entrance of a tunnel in the cliff.

There she stopped, and grinned evilly. She took an oil lamp down and lit it carefully. 'Will you not come with us, you who betrayed your king?' she asked Infadoos.

He scowled blackly. 'No. It is not fit for me to enter the Place of Death. But if any harm befalls the white men, you will answer for it with your blood, Gagool,' he answered.

She said nothing, but turned and plunged into the darkness.

The passage we found ourselves in was narrow and

black. Round our heads brushed the wings of startled
bats, but we could not see them. We followed Gagool
perhaps fifty paces into the rock; there the passage turned
sharply, and suddenly we found ourselves in the first cave.

Imagine yourself in a great cathedral, whose walls seem
to leap up and meet high over your head, and you will have
a fair idea of the size and beauty of the place we stood in.
Unlike the passage it was light. Somewhere high above us
there must have been an opening into daylight. And the

light shone softly down on the glistening white of hundreds of tall stalactites. Even as we stood there we could hear the water dripping down onto them and slowly building up those graceful pillars.

I could have stayed an hour, just to admire that wonderful hall. But Gagool was hurrying on through the cave. At the top end we came to a little square doorway, and here she stopped. She leered back at us in the gloom and asked, 'Dare you enter the Place of Death, white men?'

'This is getting distinctly creepy,' whispered Sir Henry to me. Then he motioned me forward. 'After you,' he said. 'Eldest first!'

I must admit it was one time when I would willingly have been last.

Slowly I followed the sound of Gagool's tapping stick down another dark passage. When she stopped I could see we were in another, smaller cave. But here there was very little light, so it took me some time to see what was in it.

When at last I did see, I confess I turned and ran. If Sir Henry had not caught and held me, I swear that not all the diamonds in the world would have made me go on.

The cave was half filled by a huge table. On it was something brown, and round it were seated mysterious white figures. Their forms were almost human – but somehow blurred. But at the head of the table sat the most awful figure I have ever seen. Death himself sat there, grinning from his skull at his strange guests.

The figure was a gigantic skeleton, carved from the living rock and as white as bone. In its right hand it clutched a vast spear with which it threatened the room and its occupants. It was as though it had just started up from its seat in order to dash out the life of some unfortunate wretch.

90

'Welcome to the Place of Death, white men,' crowed Gagool. 'It is bad luck to all men who enter here! Come,' she added, turning to Sir Henry. 'You who killed Twala, see where he lies.' And she led us all towards the table.

With a shock we saw that the brown object on the centre of the table was Twala's naked and seated body. Its head lay in its hands, and over it something glistened. I was puzzled at first. Then I heard a drop of water and realised that from high in the roof drops were falling straight onto the seated body.

Twala was being turned slowly, very slowly, into a stalagmite!

Then I saw that all the strange white figures who sat as guests round the table of Death were stalagmites, too. All the kings of the Kukuanas sat around me, white and still forever!

While we stood gazing in amazement at this horrible sight, Gagool was busy. She climbed upon the table and shuffled past the figures seated there. Every so often she would stop and mutter at one or other of them, as though she were talking to an old friend. Finally she stopped and crouched in front of the figure of Death. Perhaps she was offering prayers to it.

'Now, Gagool, you have promised to show us the treasure,' I called to her as she came down. It seemed time that we reminded her of our purpose.

'Are you not afraid?' she asked.

'Lead on.'

'Then here, my lords, is the secret of the Place of Death.'

With these words she turned towards the bare, smooth rock, and pointed. We could see nothing.

'Come, now – no joking!' said Sir Henry fiercely.

But it was no joke. Slowly in front of our eyes a huge slab of rock was lifting up. We could not see where it joined the walls. Nor could we see what Gagool had done to set in action the marvellous machinery that was opening it. But opening it was!

I must admit I could hardly contain my excitement as the great door swung upwards. Here at last was to be the end of our journeys! Here legend was to become fact!

Good and Sir Henry seemed to share my feelings, for as soon as the door was high enough all three of us pressed through. We were checked by Gagool's voice.

'Enter, white men,' she said. And her voice rang cold in that dismal cave. 'But before you do, know that there is a curse put on the place by the men who once dug the bright stones from the earth. Those who enter will die within the month.'

We all stopped and looked at each other. It was not easy to feel brave in that place. Then Good said, 'Oh hang it all – I'm not superstitious! And we've been through enough to get here. Come on!'

And on we went into King Solomon's Treasure House.

Beyond the door lay no cave, but a room, hacked out of the rock. It was small, and completely dark. Indeed we had to wait while Sir Henry went back down the small passage that led to it for Gagool's lamp.

What the lamplight showed us was, first, rows and rows of elephant tusks – more fine ivory than I had got in a lifetime's hunting! On the opposite wall were stacks of wooden boxes. 'Aha!' I cried. 'These will be our diamonds!'

Quickly we stove in a plank or two and thrust in our hands. But out came not diamonds but gold pieces. It was a little disappointing. Still, it meant we should not go back empty-handed.

We should have left happy enough with the gold – and perhaps it would have been better if we had. But Good, who had wandered to the dark far corner, suddenly

stumbled upon a little opening – and on the ledges inside lay three stone chests. We had found the diamonds!

I think I could have been happy for hours just feeling the smooth roundness of the uncut stones – or weighing them in my hand. Eagerly we held them against the light. We would be the richest men in the world!

Our excitement was broken by the sound of women's

voices down the passage behind us. Foulata and Gagool seemed to speak angrily. Then Foulata's voice came echoing down the rock in a shriek. Even now when I think of it that voice turns my blood cold.

'The door,' she cried. 'The door! It is closing!'

9 Back from the dead

We dropped the stones and ran. As soon as we left the chamber we could see the disaster that threatened us. Somehow Gagool had managed to touch off the mechanism which closed the door. And already the huge slab of stone was only three feet from the floor.

Silhouetted against the fast-closing doorway were two struggling figures. Foulata was struggling to hold Gagool back on our side of the door.

Even now if I shut my eyes I can see that short and desperate scene. We ran, but our feet seemed to drag slowly as they do sometimes in dreams. And as we ran we saw a knife flash in Gagool's withered hands. The next second, Foulata fell to her knees, blood streaming from a wound in her side. With a shrill shriek Gagool dived at the narrow gap still open at the bottom of the door. It seemed for a moment just wide enough for her shrivelled body to crawl through. But no – down came the rock, ton upon ton of it. For a second Gagool was pinned alive under it. Then there was a horrible scream that rose up and up – and suddenly stopped. And just as we hurled ourselves at it the door slid firmly against the bedrock.

Like an insect crushed under a giant tread, Gagool the ancient, the wise, the evil, was dead.

Sir Henry and I leaned panting against the rock. Good bent swiftly over the form of Foulata. I saw him lift up her head and cradle it gently for a moment. Then a kind of sob came from him. 'She is dead!' he said, and there were tears in his voice. 'The witch has murdered her. And she tried to save us!'

'Well,' I answered, 'we will be joining her soon, I think. This door will never open for us again – and I saw no other.'

'So that was why the old witch led us here!' said Sir Henry. 'It was a trap all the time.'

'And we are in it,' I added. 'We have enough food for one meal, and enough light for half an hour, I should guess. If there is another way out – and I doubt it – we had better use the last of our light to look for it.'

So dismally we began to pace round our little prison. Even Good was persuaded to leave his grieving over poor Foulata, and search with us.

I think we peered into and tapped and felt every inch of the walls and floor and ceiling. There was not much to find. The place was obviously only a store, and was no larger than it need have been. Soon we were all back at the door, staring silently at the mass of rock that cut us off from the world. We knew it was the only door – and we knew that no-one inside or outside it could ever open it.

We sat upon the hard ground and ate and drank. There seemed little point in it, but there was nothing else to do.

'How wretched to have been through all that we have been through, only to die in a hole like this,' said Sir Henry. And as he spoke the words, our little lamp flickered and went out. The darkness was total.

I am not sure how long we sat there. Hours, certainly, for I think we all slept a little – but with the darkness all sense of time left us. Slowly, though, an idea was coming to me. Something about our prison seemed wrong. Something was not quite as it should be. And then I had it. The air! We had been hours in a tightly sealed room – yet the air was still fresh. From somewhere, air must be reaching the room, and if we could find the draught it might be that there was an escape after all.

At once we began our search again – only this time feeling gently into every corner for any movement of the air. It was a painful business, as we kept on banging into each other and the chests. I was already beginning after an hour or so to lose even the shred of hope the idea had given. But Good carried on searching; and suddenly he called out, 'Here, I think! There's just a faint draught on the floor!'

There was! And when we struck the rock there it sounded hollow! With tremendous excitement we began to clear away the dust around the area. At last we could all feel the faint outlines of a tightly-fitting trapdoor, and a stone ring to pull it by.

Only Sir Henry's strength could have opened it – but with a heaving and a cracking of muscles, up it came. We lit a match and peered in. There, leading down into the darkness, was a flight of stone steps.

Sir Henry and the Captain were already lowering themselves in, when I called, 'What about the diamonds?'

'Hang the diamonds,' boomed Sir Henry's voice from underground. 'I just want to get out of this place!'

I must admit I rather agreed with him. Still, I stuck my hand quickly into the chest in the dark, and pocketed a couple of handfuls of stones. Then we set off down the steps. For all we knew they led nowhere – but at least this was better than sitting and waiting to die.

It was soon clear that we were wandering in something like a maze. The steps soon gave way to a narrow tunnel which sloped down; and we had not gone far before it forked, and then forked again. With no guide or map we had to trust to luck, and it was not long before we felt utterly lost.

I had the impression that we were generally walking downhill, rather than up. But we could have been in the heart of the mountain for all I knew. Hours of walking and resting went by. And then we began to be aware of the distant sound of running water.

All of us were thirsty, so we used the sound to guide us. Whenever we came to a turning we went that way where the sound of water seemed loudest. And pretty soon the noise had grown into a roar loud enough to drown our voices. We were going along slowly, one behind the other, and Good was leading. Suddenly there was a splash and a cry. He had fallen in!

Anxiously we stood still and called to him. After a while his voice came back to us, some way ahead.

'Light a match!' he called. 'I can't see where you are, and I shall have to swim back to you.'

One of the precious handful of matches we had was lit, and by its light we could see the Captain. He was clinging to a rock some way off the bank of a great, black river.

With a flurry of water he launched himself back towards the edge. The river ran deep, fast and cold, and for a moment it seemed he would be swept away. Then we managed to catch at him and haul him out.

The water was sweet and cold to drink, and it refreshed us. But Good was now cold and shivering, and I think we all realised as we trudged away from the river that we were no nearer to safety. Every turning was a matter of

chance – and only chance would ever bring us out into the daylight again.

For many more hours we walked. Now we barely spoke, and our feet moved wearily. So it happened that we did not at first notice the change in the tunnel. It had run evenly through the rock, always high enough to walk in comfort. Now it started to close slowly in on us. And then we saw we were walking on packed earth, not rock.

'Are my eyes playing tricks?' asked Good. 'Or is that really a speck of light?'

It was! Nearer grew the light, narrower grew the tunnel. We had to crawl and struggle through the last few feet. Then with a burst we were out, sitting together on a grass bank.

Before we had time to congratulate each other on our escape, the bank gave way beneath us and sent us all tumbling down a steep slope. When we came to rest we

found that we were sitting at the very bottom of the great pit, by the Silent Ones. Three hundred feet of steep clay, with odd grassy ledges like the one we had sat on, loomed over us.

Bruised and exhausted as we were, it was dark before we had struggled to the rim. Tired, we flopped onto the stones of Solomon's Great Road. Ahead a camp fire burned, and from it a figure came towards us. It was old Infadoos!

'My lords, my lords!' he cried when he saw us. 'You are come back from the dead!

And that is how we felt, too.

Our last days amongst the Kukuanas were pleasant, if sad. Ignosi would have had us stay, but when we reminded him how eager he had been to get back to his own land, he understood that we must part.

We went back once to the Mines – but there was no sign of the hole out of which we had escaped. Nor could we have hoped to find a way back through that maze. For some time, too, we hunted for the secret of the door. Some kind of hidden spring must have been there, but it was beyond us to find it. In any case, I think I should not have cared to step over the crushed remains of Gagool into that chamber again.

So we left those diamonds that would never sparkle in the light – left them in the dark with the bones of poor, faithful Foulata. I doubt if any beauty ever had so rich a tomb!

At last it was time for us to leave the land of the Kukuanas.

It was a fine scene, our departure. Ignosi the king stood grandly among his people. He looked fine and magnificent

Farewell to 'Beautiful White Legs'

as he made his farewells to us – but I think that secretly he was moved to think that he would never see us again. We had a great deal to remember together.

Many fine things he said to us. And the people pressed around for their last glimpse of the 'white men from the stars'. At last, when he had finished, a girl came from the crowd, knelt in front of Captain Good, and presented him with a bunch of white lilies. They were beautiful. Then she timidly asked, 'My lord, will you grant one last sight of your beautiful white legs before you leave us?'

'No, devil take it!' said Good. He had had quite enough of that, I think.

But Sir Henry joined in. 'Come on, Good. There's a good fellow! Surely you can't refuse a lady?'

So Captain Good was persuaded to roll his trouser legs up – and up they stayed until the Kraal was far behind us and the last curious Kukuana had stopped following to admire them.

And that, really, is the end of our adventures. I have told them as I promised Sir Henry I would before he sailed back to England. Captain Good sailed with him – oh, and I must not forget to tell you that a third man sailed with them both.

When we left the land of the Kukuanas we did not come back over the Breasts of Sheba. Instead we crossed the Suliman Mountains further north, where there was an easy pass – and a rich oasis out in the desert. And in the oasis, with a broken leg that had prevented him leaving it, was none other than 'Mr. Neville'. George Curtis was found at last! Two years he had spent there, with his native hunter – and I think the poor fellow had given up hope of ever escaping. Never have I seen two happier men

than Sir Henry and his younger brother, out in that green oasis.

The two handfuls of diamonds I brought out proved to be of such quality that there was enough to make the four of us wealthy men – so George Curtis found his fortune after all.

And I – well, after all these years, Africa suits me. But I am glad enough to be able to retire from elephant hunting. I have bought myself a pleasant house in Durban. And now that I have got this confounded story-telling done, I intend to enjoy my retirement in peace.

Piccolo Adventure Library

The Adventures of Ulysses 50p

Across dangerous seas and strange lands peopled by giants and
monsters, Ulysses and his crew battle with the angry god
Poseidon as they struggle home from the Trojan Wars – to
fight traitors and recover a kingdom.

The Last of the Mohicans 50p

The great adventure of the wild country with Hawkeye the
Deerslayer and Chingachgook, Last of the Mohicans. Indian
fighting, trail blazing, long rifle and war hatchet fill these
exciting days of the French-Indian Wars.

20,000 Leagues Under the Sea 50p

The thrilling story of Captain Nemo and his extraordinary
submarine *Nautilus* journeying through the strange and
hazardous depths beneath the oceans.

Treasure Island 50p

The famous adventures of Jim Hawkins and the crew of the
Hispaniola in search of buried treasure and locked in a battle of
wits and cutlasses with Long John Silver and his villainous
pirates.

Alexander Barrie
Fly for Three Lives 45p

When Jonathan got a holiday job at Lonehead Flying Field, he expected a few enjoyable weeks of messing about with planes and a couple of flying lessons.

But when the sinister Mr Barrington-Ward appeared, Jon was suddenly launched into real airborne adventure – stolen planes, flying bullets and a cut-throat crew of political gangsters . . .

Operation Midnight 45p

It seemed as if it would never stop raining at Lonehead Flying Field. Then an urgent call from the Ministry of Defence plunged Johnathan and the rest of the team into a new adventure. 'Operation Midnight' – the code name for a mission to Africa to rescue Ephraim Demir from his border hideout. The mission became more and more dangerous as Johnathan found himself at the centre of a thrilling prison rescue . . .

Let Them All Starve 45p

Mambay is a poor country and when the rain stopped the people were dying like flies. Mrs Kidwallader-Jones was determined to help but the relief supplies were just not getting through. So she hired Jonathan and his Lonehead Flying Field chums to fly out to Africa to find out why . . .